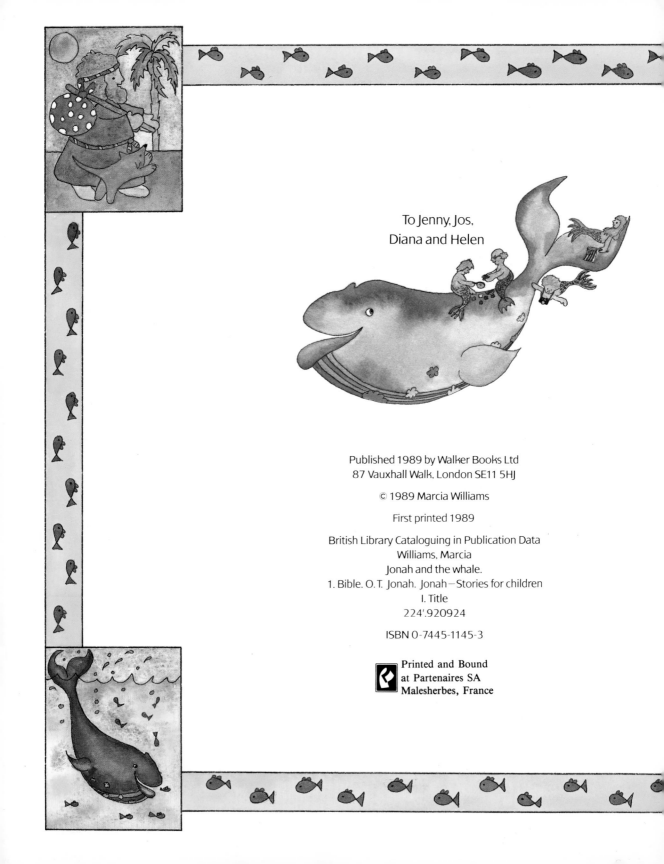

To Jenny, Jos,
Diana and Helen

Published 1989 by Walker Books Ltd
87 Vauxhall Walk, London SE11 5HJ

© 1989 Marcia Williams

First printed 1989

British Library Cataloguing in Publication Data
Williams, Marcia
Jonah and the whale.
1. Bible. O. T. Jonah. Jonah – Stories for children
I. Title
224′.920924

ISBN 0-7445-1145-3

Printed and Bound
at Partenaires SA
Malesherbes, France

JONAH
AND THE
WHALE

WRITTEN AND ILLUSTRATED BY
MARCIA WILLIAMS

WALKER BOOKS
LONDON

Many, many moons ago

in a land of deserts and date palms

God spoke to a man named Jonah.

"Arise," He said, "and go to Nineveh.

Warn the people against their wickedness,

for if they do not change their ways

I shall destroy their city."

But Jonah did not believe God would do this.

He decided to run away, and not go to Nineveh.

He found a ship travelling to Tarshish,

in the opposite direction from Nineveh.

He paid his fare and went on board.

This angered God,

so He sent a tempestuous storm.

The howling wind tore at the ship's sail.

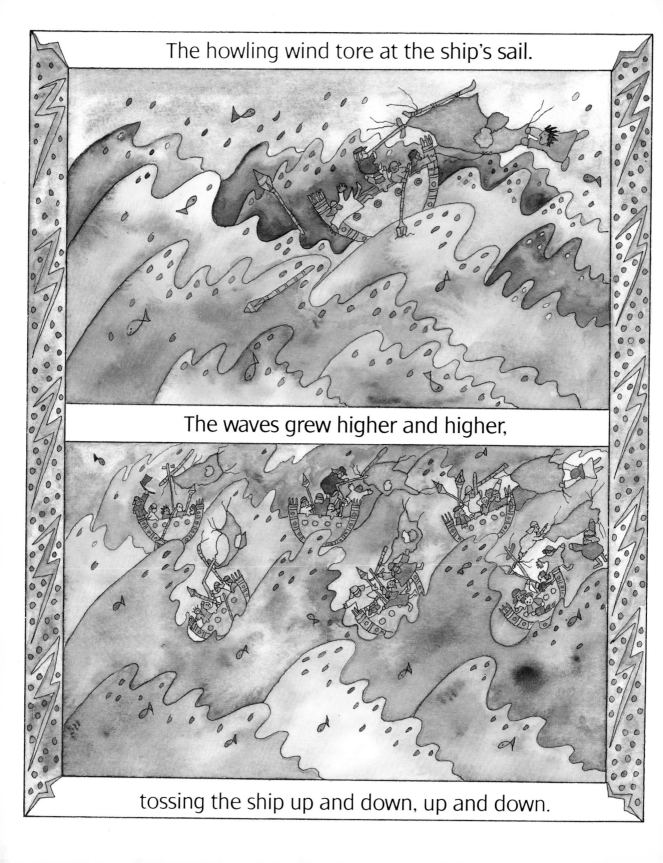

The waves grew higher and higher,

tossing the ship up and down, up and down.

The sailors feared that the ship would break in two.

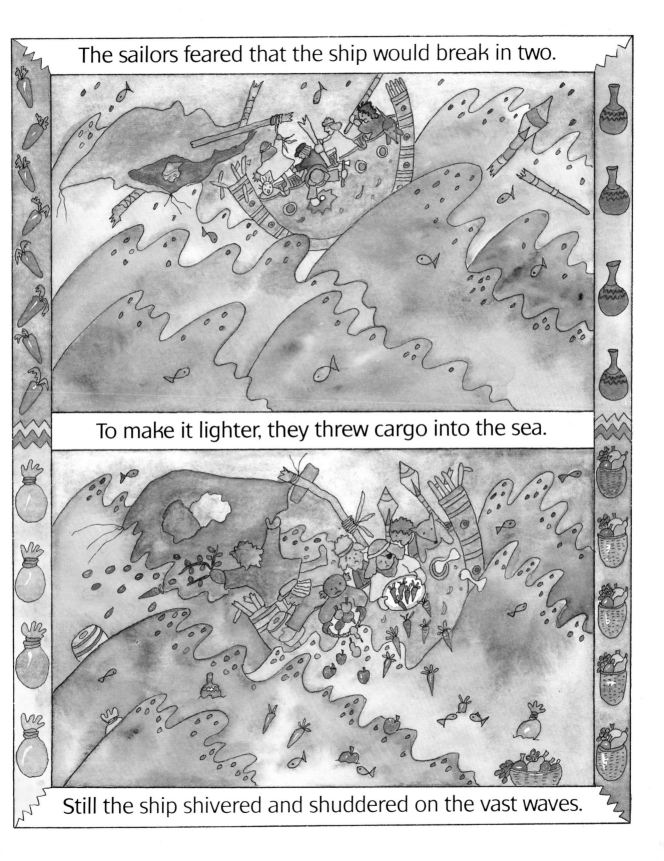

To make it lighter, they threw cargo into the sea.

Still the ship shivered and shuddered on the vast waves.

Above deck the sailors prayed to their gods

while below, Jonah slept

until the captain woke him.

"Jonah," he said, "pray to your God to save us!"

Though Jonah prayed, the storm grew even fiercer.

The sailors and their captain were terrified.

Then Jonah told them that God had sent the storm

because he had not gone to Nineveh.

"If I give myself to the sea," said Jonah,

"I'm sure the waters will be calm again."

The sailors did not want Jonah to drown

and they tried hard to row to land.

But in vain, for the sea became even wilder.

So, sadly, they threw Jonah overboard.

Instantly the raging waters grew calm.

Fearing for Jonah's life,

the sailors prayed to God for forgiveness.

Then they set sail again for Tarshish

on the still, clear waters.

But Jonah did not drown.

At first he floated.

Then he became caught in weeds.

Jonah was dragged

into the depths of the sea.

Just as he felt he was about to die,

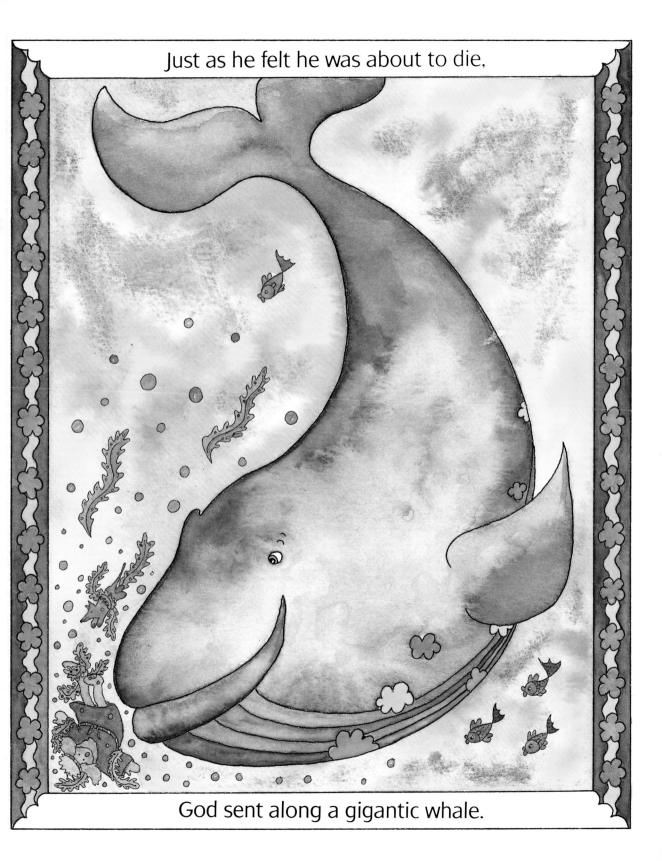

God sent along a gigantic whale.

The whale swallowed Jonah whole.

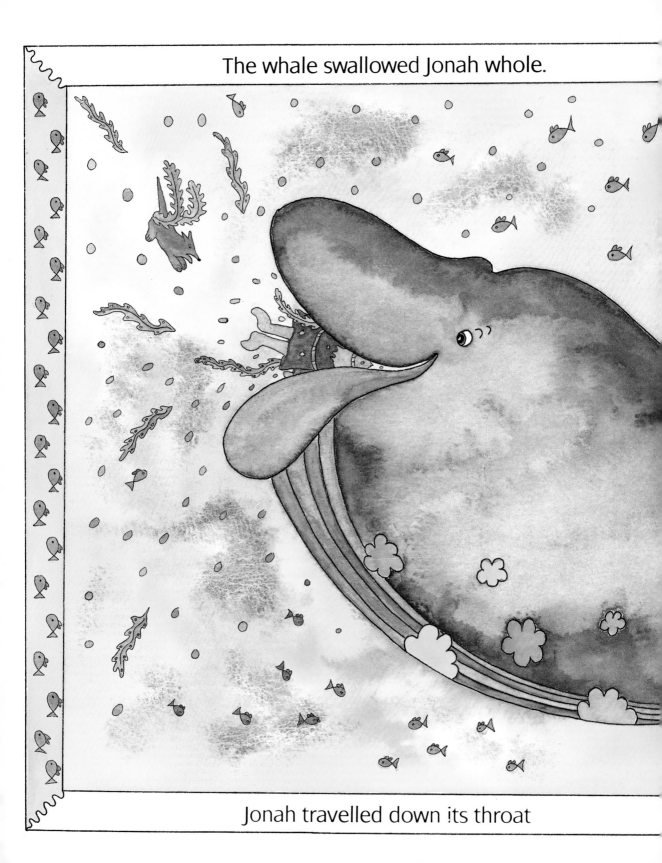

Jonah travelled down its throat

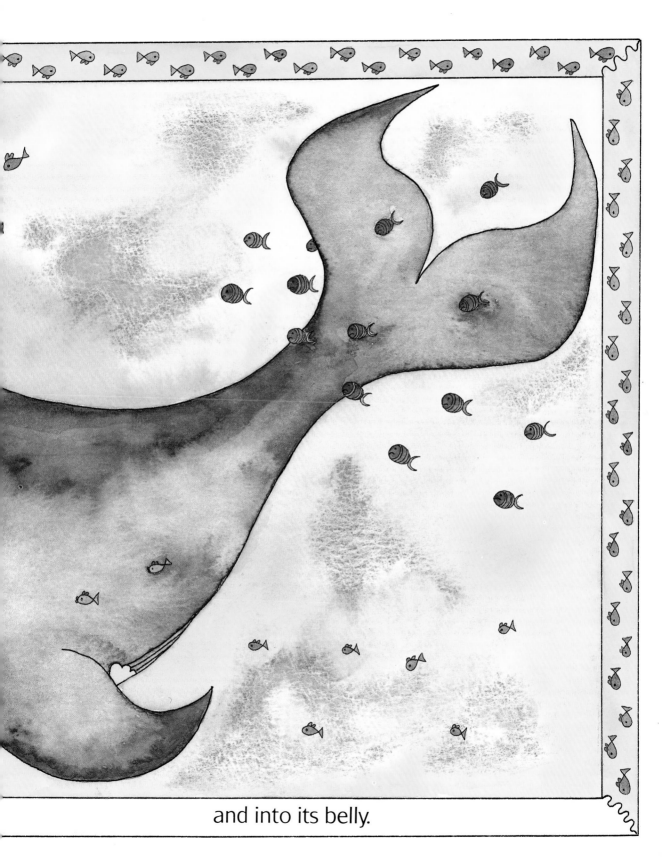

and into its belly.

It was cold and dark and Jonah was afraid.

Three days and three nights passed.

Sometimes Jonah slept,

but mostly he prayed to God to forgive him.

At last God took pity on Jonah

and told the whale to spit him out.

Jonah landed on the earth with a bump.

He was very shaken

and could hardly stand on his feet,

but he was glad to be on dry land.

Then God spoke to Jonah again.

"Go to Nineveh," He said, "and warn the people

that in forty days their city will be destroyed

unless they become good and kind."

This time Jonah obeyed God.

He travelled to Nineveh and cried out God's warning.

The King and people of Nineveh believed Jonah.

They put on sackcloth and promised to repent.

When God saw this he was happy to spare them,

and Jonah and everyone who lived in Nineveh rejoiced.